Caring for My Pet

Turtle

**Lynn Hamilton
and Katie Gillespie**

MEDIA ENHANCED BOOKS
AV2
BY WEIGL™
ADDED VALUE · AUDIO VISUAL

www.av2books.com

AV² provides enriched content that supplements and complements this book. Weigl's AV² books strive to create inspired learning and engage young minds in a total learning experience.

Your AV² Media Enhanced books come alive with...

Audio
Listen to sections of the book read aloud.

Key Words
Study vocabulary, and complete a matching word activity.

Video
Watch informative video clips.

Quizzes
Test your knowledge.

Go to www.av2books.com, and enter this book's unique code.

BOOK CODE

X495736

Embedded Weblinks
Gain additional information for research.

Slide Show
View images and captions, and prepare a presentation.

AV² by Weigl brings you media enhanced books that support active learning.

Try This!
Complete activities and hands-on experiments.

... and much, much more!

Published by AV² by Weigl
350 5th Avenue, 59th Floor
New York, NY 10118
Websites: www.av2books.com   www.weigl.com

Library of Congress Cataloging-in-Publication Data

Hamilton, Lynn, 1964- author.
[Turtle (AV2 by Weigl)]
Turtle / Lynn Hamilton and Katie Gillespie.
   pages cm. -- (Caring for my pet)
Includes bibliographical references.
ISBN 978-1-4896-2974-6 (hard cover : alk. paper) -- ISBN 978-1-4896-2975-3 (soft cover : alk. paper) -- ISBN 978-1-4896-2976-0 (single user ebook) -- ISBN 978-1-4896-2977-7 (multi-user ebook)
1. Turtles as pets--Juvenile literature. I. Gillespie, Katie, author. II. Title. III. Series: Caring for my pet.
SF459.T8H342 2016
639.3'92--dc23
                    2014041418

Printed in the United States of America in North Mankato, Minnesota
1 2 3 4 5 6 7 8 9 0 18 17 16 15 14

112014
WEP311214

Project Coordinator: Katie Gillespie
Designer: Mandy Christiansen

Every reasonable effort has been made to trace ownership and to obtain permission to reprint copyright material. The publishers would be pleased to have any errors or omissions brought to their attention so that they may be corrected in subsequent printings.

Weigl acknowledges Getty Images and iStock as its primary image suppliers for this title.

Caring for My Pet

Turtle

Contents

A Turtle World

There are many different kinds of turtles, each with their own names. Turtles that live on land are called tortoises. Fresh water turtles are called aquatic, or water, turtles. Turtles that live in the ocean are known as sea turtles. These interesting animals have fascinated people for hundreds of years.

Turtles are most easily recognized for the shells they carry on their backs. They are also well known for moving slowly on land. Even though they do not bark, purr, or cuddle like some animals, turtles make great pets. Each turtle has a personality and routine all her own. Keeping a turtle as a pet is a unique way to welcome a piece of nature into your life.

Red-eared sliders are one of the most *popular* turtle pets.

There are about **300 known species** of turtles.

Turtles belong to the **Testudinidae** family.

Some turtles may **grow** until age **50**.

Turtle **shells** have between **59** and **61 bones**.

Turtles are popular pets in the United States. More than one million homes across the country have at least one pet turtle.

Turtles through Time

Turtles are a fascinating link to the past. The first turtles lived about 220 million years ago. They shared the Earth with dinosaurs. We can learn about these turtles from their **fossils**. Today's turtles have many of the same qualities as their ancestors. However, there are some significant differences. Unlike present-day turtles, ancient turtles had teeth. They also had spiny armor covering their tails and necks, and were unable to pull their necks inside of their shells.

Over time, turtles have changed to suit their environments. Land turtles have strong, thick shells. These shells help to protect them from dangerous **predators**. Sea turtles are good swimmers, thanks to their flat shells and paddle-like legs.

Make sure the turtle you choose is legal in your area. Check with game or wildlife authorities before buying your pet.

Turtles belong to a group called reptiles. This means they have lungs, scales, and lay their eggs on land. Reptiles are also cold-blooded. Other animals belonging to this group include lizards, snakes, alligators, and crocodiles.

Turtles have been connected to people for a very long time. These animals were once used for food during long trips across the ocean. People have made turtle shells into jewelry. Some Native American creation stories even feature turtles. Today, they are also sold as pets.

Turtles can be found on **every continent** except **Antarctica**.

The **oldest** turtle fossils were found in **China**.

CHINA

A **turtle's shell** has two parts called the **carapace** (top) and the **plastron** (bottom).

Many populations of sea turtles are endangered due to human activities. Special laws have been made to help protect these animals.

Pet Profile

There are many kinds of turtles. Each has different needs. To live long, happy lives, pet turtles must be cared for properly. Some turtles are mainly land animals, while others are more often found in the water. Most turtles spend their time both on land and in water. It is important to provide your pet turtle with a tank that suits him. Turtles that **hibernate** will need a place to do so safely. Your pet will also require regular grooming, feeding, and visits to the **veterinarian**.

Red-Eared Sliders

- Can live for more than 25 years
- Are active during the day
- Grow about 11 or 12 inches (28 or 30 centimeters) long
- Have olive-green skin with yellow markings
- Have red patches near the ears
- Like to swim, but need dry land as well
- May be aggressive toward people or other turtles

Spotted Turtles

- Are mostly **carnivorous**
- Grow about 5 inches (13 cm) long
- Have a black carapace with yellow spots
- Have brown eyes if male and yellow eyes if female
- Like to swim
- May be aggressive toward other turtles

Musk Turtles

- Are mostly carnivorous
- Grow about 4 to 6 inches (10 to 15 cm) long
- Can climb well
- Spray a smelly liquid when upset
- May be aggressive toward other turtles
- Are closely related to mud turtles

Box Turtles

- Eat both meat and plants
- Can live between 30 and 40 years
- Grow about 6 to 8 inches (15 to 20 cm) long
- Have a black or brown carapace with yellow, brown, and orange markings
- Are able to tuck their arms and legs inside their hinged shell

Painted Turtles

- Can live for about 20 years
- Are active during the day
- Grow about 8 to 10 inches (20 to 25 cm) long
- Have some red markings on their carapace and legs
- Have yellow markings on their head
- Need an aquarium with a **basking** surface

Wood Turtles

- Can live for at least 25 years
- Grow about 10 inches (25 cm) long
- Have **scutes** in the shape of four-sided peaks
- Enjoy climbing and digging
- May learn to recognize their owner
- Need both land and water areas in their tank

Picking Your Pet

Caring for a pet turtle is a big responsibility. Owners must be familiar with turtle behavior. They also have to recreate their pet's natural environment. It is important to know that turtles will hide in their shells if they are scared. However, they can also be active animals that are fun to watch. If you want to become a turtle owner, you will need to learn all about making a healthy home for your pet.

Can I Provide a Good Home for a Turtle?

Turtles require clean homes with enough room for their activities. If the climate is suitable, your pet turtle may spend some time outside. However, it is not safe to release your pet into nature. The local environment may not be a good fit for her, and she may not be able to survive in the outdoor climate.

The best place for your turtle is inside her tank, whether it is an indoor aquarium or an outdoor enclosure. The temperature should be carefully controlled. Make sure that the tank is placed on a sturdy surface away from potential dangers. Keep your turtle protected from other pets, such as cats, dogs, snakes, rodents, and birds.

🐾 Turtles carry a dangerous bacteria called salmonella, which can make young children sick. For their safety, children under age five should not keep turtles as pets.

What Will a Turtle Cost?

Some turtles are quite affordable. However, it can be expensive to set up your pet's tank. Other costs include food, cleaning products, and tank supplies. You may need to buy medicine if your turtle gets sick. She will also require yearly visits to the veterinarian.

Am I Ready to Care for a Turtle?

Before deciding to become a turtle owner, make sure you have time in your schedule to spend with your pet. You will need to care for her every day. A routine will be very important. If you are away from home, someone reliable will need to look after your turtle.

The *largest* freshwater turtle in *North America* is the *alligator snapping turtle.*

Some turtles lay **oblong-shaped** eggs, while others lay **round** eggs.

Turtles have **no external** ears.

Both **rare** and **common** turtles are kept as pets.

The **FASTEST** turtles can swim up to **22 miles** per hour. (35 kilometers per hour)

Even though members of the same species may be seen together, turtles are not social animals. They do not need to share their home with other turtles to be happy.

Life Cycle

Some turtles are born and raised in captivity. Others are collected from nature and sold as pets. Your turtle will have different needs throughout his life. Learning more about each stage of your turtle's development will help you provide him with the best possible care.

Eggs

Female turtles dig a hole to lay their eggs inside. It is usually in a sunny spot. They cover the eggs with plant matter and soil to keep them warm and protected. Depending on their species, turtles lay anywhere from a few eggs to hundreds of eggs. They take about two to three months to hatch. Turtle breeders may place eggs inside an **incubator**. This keeps them safe from the cold and from predators. In nature, only a few turtles out of hundreds may survive to maturity.

Hatchlings

Hatchlings break out of their eggs using a sharp point on the tip of their beak-like jaw. This is called an egg tooth. It falls off once the turtle has hatched from its shell. The hatching process can take minutes, hours, or even a few days. Once hatched, baby turtles must dig up through their protective coverings to reach the surface.

Growth and Maturity

Turtles have growth rings on their shells. While they do not tell a turtle's age, growth rings do provide information about his growing stages. At age three, turtles are about one-third of their adult size. By age six, they are two-thirds grown. A turtle's life span depends on many factors. His species, environment, and the quality of the care he receives will all impact how long a turtle lives.

Baby Turtles

Baby turtles have a special yolk sac attached to their plastron. They feed off this for about one week after birth. The yolk sac detaches from their body when it is no longer needed. Baby turtles need special nutrition to help their shells properly develop. They should be kept in their own enclosure, away from adult turtles.

Tanks for Turtles

Some turtles may be kept outside during the warm months of summer. If you keep your pet turtle outdoors, she will need an enclosure covered in wire mesh. This will help protect her from outdoor predators. If you keep your pet indoors, an aquarium or sturdy plastic container is a good choice of home.

Cover the bottom of your turtle's tank in gravel or artificial grass. You can find these materials at a pet store. Choose the materials you place in your turtle's home carefully. Some may be difficult to keep clean. Others may be small enough for her to swallow, which can be dangerous. Find out if your turtle needs a place to dig and burrow. Some species like to have places to hide. You can put a hollowed log or a wooden box in your turtle's tank for this purpose.

The amount of water in your turtle's tank depends on her size. For every 1 inch (2.5 cm) of her length, there should be about 10 gallons (38 liters) of water.

Galapagos tortoises travel about **18 times slower** than people.

A turtle's feet are usually **webbed**, while a tortoise's feet are **round** and **stumpy**.

Some tortoise *hatchlings* are about the same size as a *grape*.

Your pet's drinking **water** should be changed **once a day**.

Some **plants** can be **poisonous** to turtles.

Warm nest temperatures make more **female** turtles and **cool** nest temperatures make more **male** turtles.

Turtles have very specific needs. They require sunlight or lighting with ultraviolet B (UVB) rays to stay healthy. The lighting in your turtle's tank should match the natural changes in sunlight. Make sure your pet has a water container for swimming or wading and a dry surface for basking. She will need a ramp to climb out of the water. It is also a good idea to put a heating light above one end of her basking area.

Thermometers can help you to regulate the temperature in your turtle's tank. They tell you how hot or cold the air and water are inside your turtle's home. A special heater will keep the water warm, and a filter will keep it clean. Place a cover over your pet's enclosure as well. This will keep her safe from other family pets or small children.

Turtle Treats

Turtles can be picky about their food. Since it is important for your pet to eat a healthy mix of foods, you should cut his meals up into small pieces. This will stop him from picking out his favorite foods and ensure he gets a varied diet. Include fruits and vegetables, such as blueberries, cantaloupes, carrots, peas, and cucumbers in your pet's meals. Always wash these kinds of foods before feeding them to your turtle.

Young turtles must be fed every day. Older turtles only need feeding around three times a week.

Some turtles prefer more meat in their diet. You can give your turtle foods such as insects, snails, crayfish, trout, and freshwater shrimp. Turtles also need calcium in their diet. Calcium helps keep their bones and shells healthy. You can find calcium, vitamin, and other mineral **supplements** at pet stores.

Your pet turtle may overeat. Watch for signs that he is overweight. These include a bulging tail, underside, and legs. To make sure that your turtle stays healthy, talk to your veterinarian. She can suggest the right foods for your pet, as well as a suitable feeding schedule. It is also a good idea to separate land and water turtles during feeding times. This will keep them from biting one another when reaching for food.

Most turtles eat both plants and animals. Worms should always be rinsed before you give them to your pet.

Turtles will only **hibernate** if they are not fed for **several days**. ZZZ ZZZ

About **50** to **80** **percent** of a **young** turtle's diet should be **meat**.

Spinach causes **kidney problems** in turtles.

Tortoises that see in **color** love **red** foods.

Never feed your pet **rhubarb leaves** because they are **poisonous** to turtles.

Shells and Such

Turtles have many traits that are well suited to their particular way of life. Knowing more about your turtle's physical features will help you be a better pet owner. Understanding how your pet's body works and **adapts** to the world around her will allow you to create a suitable home to meet her needs.

Shell

A turtle's carapace is joined to her plastron by bony bridges. The surface of her shell is made of **keratin**. The bony plates of the shell are called scutes.

Tail

One way to tell male and female turtles apart is by their tails. Generally, males have thicker, longer, and more pointed tails than females.

Skin

Turtles have scales all over their skin. These scales help prevent moisture loss.

Smell

Turtles have an excellent sense of smell. They use it to find and choose their food. Water turtles can even smell underwater.

Eyes

Turtles have very good eyesight. They can spot food or predators from a distance.

Jaws

Turtles have strong jaws with sharp edges. These edges are used for crushing food.

Eardrums

A turtle's eardrums are just behind her cheeks, under the skin. Turtles can hear low, deep sounds.

Turtle Polish

It is essential to keep your pet turtle's home clean. One way to reduce mess is to feed your turtle in a small, separate container or tank. This will help to keep his main tank clean. It is important to remove any uneaten food or waste on a regular basis.

The water in your pet's aquarium must be changed often as well. Placing a filter in the tank is a good way to keep the water clean. If using a filter, you will not have to change the water as frequently. Be sure to check and clean the filter when needed.

Your pet's entire aquarium should be cleaned about every two to four weeks. To do this, first move your turtle to a temporary container. He should not stay in the tank while you clean it out.

You should never paint your pet turtle's shell. This can be very dangerous to his health.

Some **tortoises** only walk **0.5 miles per hour**. (0.8 km per hour)

Green sea turtles can lay clutches of more than *200 eggs*.

Many turtles have an **average life span** of **20 to 30 years** or more.

Some turtles use **their jaws** to **clean** one another.

The **biggest** turtle ever measured was about **9 feet** in length. (3 meters)

Any lining materials should either be washed or replaced. Use a safe cleanser for the aquarium glass, rocks, and any other surfaces. Make sure to rinse everything well. There should be no traces of cleanser left when you put your turtle back in the tank.

Just like human fingernails, a turtle's claws never stop growing. His beak is always growing, too. Long claws can keep your turtle from walking properly. If his beak is overgrown, he may have difficulty chewing. Your pet's daily activities will wear down his claws and jaw a little, but this may not be enough. If your turtle's claws or beak get too long, take him to a veterinarian for trimming.

Healthy and Happy

When choosing a pet turtle, there are many factors to consider. Watch for signs that the turtle is healthy, such as clear eyes, and a good appetite. Her shell should be firm, with few cracks.

Healthy turtles should also be able to breathe easily with a closed mouth. When you pick her up, the turtle should feel solid, not light. Check the folds of her skin for **parasites**. Water turtles should be able to swim easily below the surface. Giving your new pet a clean home and keeping her diet well balanced will help her stay happy and healthy.

As long as your turtle is healthy, she will only need to go to the vet once a year for a checkup.

As you and your pet become more familiar with each other, you will learn to observe her behavior. Soon, you will know which appearances are normal. Watch for any changes that could indicate illness. Does your pet have swollen or runny eyes? Has her appetite changed? Sores, swelling, unusual breathing sounds, or a softening shell are all symptoms that your turtle may be sick. Take her to a veterinarian if you notice any of these conditions.

One of the most common turtle illnesses is **fungus**. Fungus can grow in cracks or injuries on your turtle's shell. It will look like a cottony white film on the surface of your pet. Be very careful not to drop your turtle, as this may crack her shell.

Not all problems require a visit to the veterinarian. You can take care of simple issues at home. For instance, if your turtle flips over onto her shell, she may not be able to right herself. You can help by turning her over gently.

Never let your pet turtle wander around on grass that has been treated with chemicals. This can make her very ill.

Most tortoise shells are **high and domed**, except for the **flat shells** of pancake tortoises.

Most turtles have **short tails**.

All turtles lay their eggs **on land**.

You can tell the *two main groups* of turtles apart by *their necks*.

There are **reports** of tortoises living in captivity for **more than 100** years.

Turtle Behavior

Not all turtles get along with other turtles. Before adding a second turtle to your tank, find out if your pet is aggressive or not. If he enjoys company, you may add another turtle to the tank. The more turtles you have, the larger their tank will need to be. To help prevent the spread of disease, you should **quarantine** the new turtle. Keep him separated from any other pets for the first four weeks. This will make sure he is not sick.

Turtles may get sick if they are under stress. To avoid disturbing your turtle, keep him away from loud noises and do not tap on the glass of his tank.

Most turtles do not like to be handled. Signs that your turtle does not enjoy being held may include kicking, biting, or tucking into his shell. It is usually best to hold your turtle only when necessary. You can pick him up carefully during cleaning times or to check his health.

If your pet is small, he can be held in the palm of your hand. Guard small turtles with your hand to prevent them from falling accidentally. Larger turtles can be lifted by placing one hand on either side of their body. To pick up a large turtle, put your thumbs on the carapace and your fingers under the plastron. Land turtles are more likely to enjoy physical contact than water turtles. Land turtles may like to have their shell or head stroked.

Pet Peeves

Turtles do not like:
- tapping on the tank's glass
- loud noises
- dirty water
- too much attention
- car rides
- having their shells painted

Some turtles **dive up** to **3,000 feet below** the ocean surface. (900 m)

Most **turtle eggs** take **45 to 75 days** to hatch.

The **biggest** soft-shell turtles have **shells** weighing up to **309 pounds**. (140 kilograms)

Turtles prefer to keep their feet on the ground. They feel safer having the security of a surface under their feet.

Turtle Tales

People have been fascinated by turtles for many years. Turtle characters appear in several books, television shows, and movies. In 1950, the famous children's author Dr. Seuss wrote a book about turtles called *Yertle the Turtle*. In the story, King Yertle orders his kingdom to build him a throne from their shells. Hundreds of turtles pile on top of one another, with Yertle at the top. When one small turtle at the bottom of the pile decides he does not want to be part of the throne, it breaks.

Raphael, Donatello, Leonardo, and Michelangelo returned to the big screen in 2014, in *Teenage Mutant Ninja Turtles*.

Perhaps the most well known turtles are the Teenage Mutant Ninja Turtles. These four turtles gained superhero powers when a chemical spilled on them. Now, they spend their time fighting villains in New York City. The Ninja Turtles have starred in comics, television shows, and movies since the late 1980s and are still popular today.

The Tortoise and the Hare

One of the most classic stories featuring a turtle character is Aesop's Fable, "The Tortoise and the Hare." It is about a hare who brags of his speed. The hare thinks it is funny when the tortoise suggests that they race. When the race begins, the hare speeds past the tortoise. The tortoise follows slowly and steadily. Certain he will win the race, the hare decides he has time to take a nap. The tortoise passes the hare. When the hare wakes up, it is too late. The tortoise has already crossed the finish line. The moral of the story is that slow and steady wins the race.

Taken from Aesop's Fables

Aesop's Fables have been translated into almost all languages. Told around the world, these stories are an important part of children's literature.

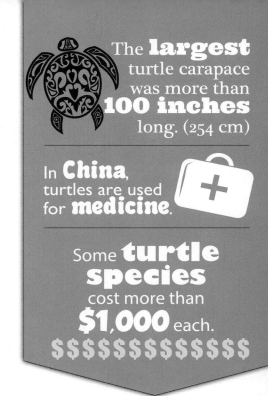

The **largest** turtle carapace was more than **100 inches** long. (254 cm)

In **China**, turtles are used for **medicine**.

Some **turtle species** cost more than **$1,000** each.
$$$$$$$$$$$$$$

Pet Puzzlers

How much do you know about turtles? If you can answer the following questions correctly, you may be ready to own a pet turtle.

1. How do a turtle's scales help keep her healthy?

By preventing moisture loss

2. Where were the oldest turtle fossils found?

China

3. How often should you feed a young turtle?

Every day

4. What is a common turtle illness?

Fungus

5. What do some turtles do when they are scared?

Hide inside their shells

6. Which parts of a turtle never stop growing?

His claws and beak

7. How long do painted turtles grow?

About 8 to 10 inches (20 to 25 cm)

8. When should you handle your pet turtle?

During cleaning times or to check his health

9. How do hatchlings break out of their eggs?

Using a sharp point on the tip of their jaw called an egg tooth

10. How many known species of turtles are there?

About 300

Turtle Tags

Before you buy your pet turtle, write down some turtle names you like. Some names may work better for a female turtle. Others may suit a male turtle. Here are just a few suggestions.

Scooter

Speedy

Myrtle

Tommy

Shelly

Peanut

Homer

Peek-a-Boo

Tucker

Sunny

Key Words

adapts: becomes used to something

basking: laying under a heat source to warm oneself

carnivorous: meat-eating

fossils: remains of ancient animals and plants from long ago found in rocks

fungus: a plant-like organism that appears as fuzz on the skin

hibernate: to spend a period of time in a sleep-like state

incubator: a container used to keep eggs warm so that they will hatch

keratin: the strong substance that makes a turtle's shell hard; the same substance found in human fingernails

parasites: organisms that live on or in other living beings

predators: animals that hunt and kill other animals for food

quarantine: temporary separation from others

scutes: bony plates on a turtle's shell

supplements: things that are added to something to make it better

veterinarian: animal doctor

Index

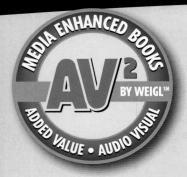

Log on to www.av2books.com

AV² by Weigl brings you media enhanced books that support active learning. Go to www.av2books.com, and enter the special code found on page 2 of this book. You will gain access to enriched and enhanced content that supplements and complements this book. Content includes video, audio, weblinks, quizzes, a slide show, and activities.

AV² Online Navigation

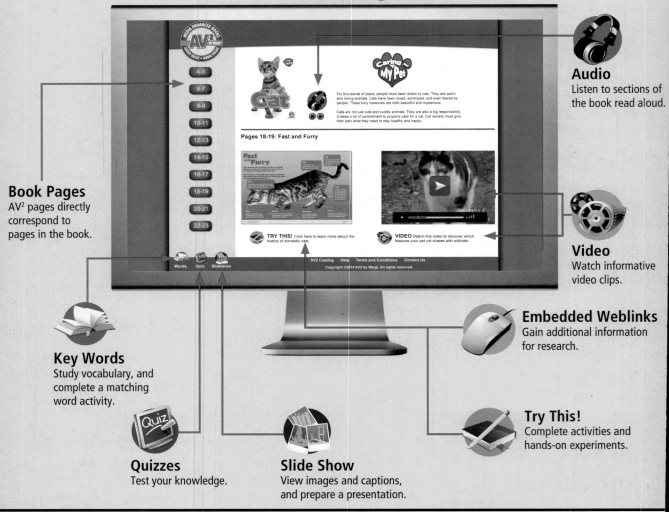

Audio
Listen to sections of the book read aloud.

Book Pages
AV² pages directly correspond to pages in the book.

Video
Watch informative video clips.

Key Words
Study vocabulary, and complete a matching word activity.

Embedded Weblinks
Gain additional information for research.

Try This!
Complete activities and hands-on experiments.

Quizzes
Test your knowledge.

Slide Show
View images and captions, and prepare a presentation.

AV² was built to bridge the gap between print and digital. We encourage you to tell us what you like and what you want to see in the future.

Sign up to be an AV² Ambassador at www.av2books.com/ambassador.

Due to the dynamic nature of the Internet, some of the URLs and activities provided as part of AV² by Weigl may have changed or ceased to exist. AV² by Weigl accepts no responsibility for any such changes. All media enhanced books are regularly monitored to update addresses and sites in a timely manner. Contact AV² by Weigl at 1-866-649-3445 or av2books@weigl.com with any questions, comments, or feedback.